This book has been
generously donated by

The Kiwanis Club of Cobourg
2003

"Young Children are Priority 1"

the Sioux

People of the Great Plains

by Anne M. Todd

Consultant:
Lydia Whirlwind Soldier, Sicangu Lakota
Indian Study Coordinator
Todd County School District
Rosebud Sioux Tribe
Mission, South Dakota

Bridgestone Books

an imprint of Capstone Press
Mankato, Minnesota

Bridgestone Books are published by Capstone Press
151 Good Counsel Drive, P.O. Box 669, Mankato, Minnesota 56002
http://www.capstone-press.com

Printed in the United States of America.

Library of Congress Cataloging-in-Publication Data
Todd, Anne M.
    Sioux : people of the Great Plains / by Anne M. Todd.
        v. cm.—(American Indian nations)
    Includes bibliographical references and index.
    Contents: The Lakota, Dakota, and Nakota—Historical life among the
    Oceti Sakowin—Who Are the Sioux—Life in a modern
    world—Sharing the old ways.
    ISBN 0-7368-1354-3 (hardcover)
    1. Dakota Indians—History—Juvenile literature. 2. Dakota
    Indians—Social life and customs—Juvenile literature. [1. Dakota
    Indians. 2. Indians of North America—Great Plains.] I. Title.
    II. American Indian nations series.
    E99.D1 T63 2003
    978.004'9752—dc21

                                                        2002002655

Editorial Credits

Bradley P. Hoehn, editor; Karen Risch, product planning editor; Kia Adams,
designer and illustrator; Wanda Winch, photo researcher

Photo Credits

Marilyn "Angel" Wynn, cover, cover inset, 4, 20 (right), 34, 40; Marilyn "Angel"
Wynn/Karl Bodmer, 10, George Catlin, 19, Mary Hill Museum, Washington,
20 (left), Utah Museum of Natural History, 44, 45; Corbis/David Muench, 9;
Stock Montage Inc./The Newberry Library, 13; *Counting Coup* by Susan
Blackwood, 14; Minnesota Historical Society/Frances Densmore, 17, Anton
Gag, 27; Capstone Press/Gary Sundermeyer, 21; Stock Montage Inc., 22, 28, 33;
Hulton Archive by Getty Images/W.H. Jackson, 24; Hulton Archive by Getty
Images, 31; Cumberland County Historical Society, Carlisle, PA/J.N. Choate
Collection, 37; photo courtesy of Virginia Driving Hawk Sneve, 38; Philbrook
Museum of Art, Tulsa, OK/Oscar Howe, 42
Special thanks to Susan Blackwood for permission to publish her painting.
Further information on this artist can be found at: *www.susanblackwood.com*

1 2 3 4 5 6 07 06 05 04 03 02

Table of Contents

Features

Lakota children participate in cultural events such as wacipis. Wacipi is the Lakota word for powwow. The Lakota often return to the reservation to celebrate their culture and heritage.

Chapter One

The Lakota, Dakota, and Nakota

Lakota, Dakota, and Nakota are three separate nations that make up an American Indian group called the Oceti Sakowin. This name means "Seven Council Fires." The Oceti Sakowin is the name used to refer to all Sioux tribes. The Oceti Sakowin also are known as the Sioux Nation. These three nations, or groups of people, act together to form one unit.

The Sioux Nation

Several ideas explain the beginning of the Sioux Nation. Some say the Oceti Sakowin came from the woodlands of Minnesota. Others say the nation's birth traces back to the Black Hills of South Dakota.

About 113,500 people belong to the Oceti Sakowin. These people share similar languages, histories, and cultures. Stories passed down teach the values, culture, and history of the Sioux Nation. Stories tell of the stars, known as the Great Spirit's holy breath, as well as the Earth and the Sun. The people of the Sioux nation seek to live in harmony with the universe. Most live in the northern plains of the United States and Canada.

The Lakota

The Lakota Nation has the largest population of the three nations. Today, about half of the 58,500 Lakota people live on reservations. A reservation is a piece of land that the U.S. government sets aside for American Indians to use without interference. Lakota reservations include Pine Ridge, Rosebud, Standing Rock, Cheyenne River, Crow Creek, and

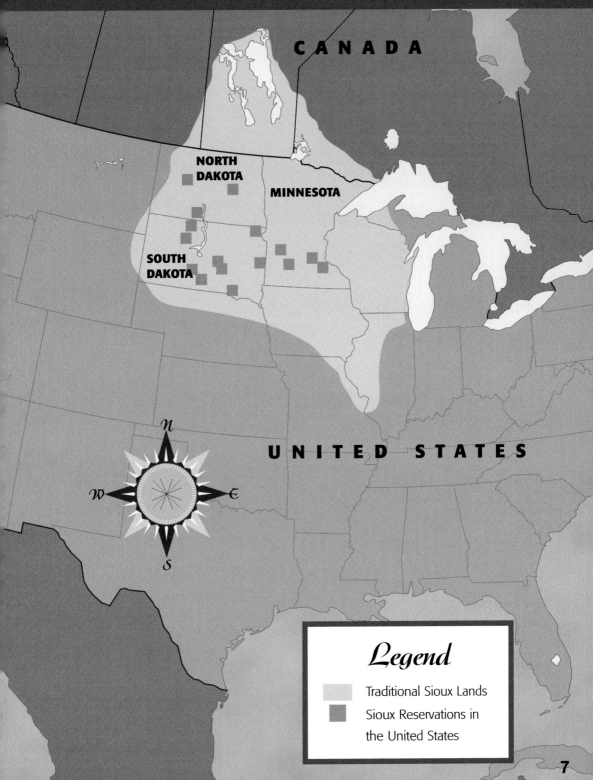

CANADA

NORTH
DAKOTA

MINNESOTA

SOUTH
DAKOTA

UNITED STATES

N

W   *E*

S

Legend

Traditional Sioux Lands

Sioux Reservations in
the United States

Lower Brulé. These reservations are located almost entirely in South Dakota. The largest Lakota reserve in Canada is the Blood Indian Reserve. A reserve is a Canadian reservation.

Almost 30,000 Lakota have left the reservations to go to college or to find work. But most of the Lakota who leave return to the reservations during the summer months. They attend cultural events such as powwows and visit family and friends. Almost all Lakota who leave the reservation in search of work return once they have retired.

The Dakota and Nakota

The population of the Dakota Nation is about 30,000. Many Dakota people leave the reservations to find work or go to college. Like the Lakota people, the Dakota often return during the summer months for cultural events or to live during their retirement. Most of the Dakota reservations are located in Minnesota. A few Dakota reservations are located in South Dakota and in North Dakota.

Fewer than 25,000 Nakota people live in the United States today. More than 14,000 Nakota live on reservations. The rest live off the reservation, usually in large cities. The Nakota also live in Canada. They have reservations in Minnesota, North Dakota, and South Dakota.

The Pine Ridge Sioux Reservation is located in South Dakota.
Much of the Great Plains looks like this scene with a lot of
open prairie land.

The Dakota word for tepee is "tipi." Buffalo skin lodge tepees were usually put up and taken down by the Sioux women. This work was their responsibilty when the tribe moved to another location.

Chapter Two

Life among the Oceti Sakowin

Around A.D. 1000, seven tribes lived in the present-day state of Minnesota around Lake Mille Lacs. These tribes included the Mdewakantons, the Wahpetons, the Wahpekutes, the Sissetons, the Yanktons, the Yanktonais, and the Tetons.

They made their homes throughout the woodlands. They hunted, fished, and harvested wild rice. People did not have to travel far from their homeland.

These original seven tribes called themselves the Oceti Sakowin. When French fur traders arrived in the 1600s, they heard an enemy tribe calling the Oceti Sakowin "nado-weisiw-eg," or "snakes." The French shortened this name to "Sioux," and the name stuck.

In the 1600s, enemy tribes such as Ojibwa and Cree began to force some of the Oceti Sakowin people west. The Lakota lived on the plains as far west as present-day Montana. The enemy tribes used guns to force the Lakota out of their territory. During this time, the Cheyenne introduced the horse to the Oceti Sakowin people. The horse greatly improved their ability to travel. The Oceti Sakowin people camped along routes the buffalo traveled. They often hunted buffalo.

The Lakota, Dakota, and Nakota

The Oceti Sakowin lands stretched as far east as present-day Wisconsin and as far west as the Rocky Mountains. The eastern tribes included the Mdewakantons, the Wahpetons, the Wahpekutes, and the Sissetons. Together, they were called the Dakota. They lived along the Minnesota River and continued to hunt and fish on the prairies and woodlands of the Midwest.

The Yankton and Yanktonais tribes, called the Nakota, lived just east of the Missouri River. The Teton tribe, called the Lakota, lived west of the Missouri River. The Lakota land stretched throughout the Black Hills of South Dakota to the Big Horn Mountains in Wyoming and Montana. The Lakota consisted of seven separate tribes including the Oglala, Brulé, Hunkpapa, Miniconjous, Two Kettle, Sans Arc, and Blackfeet. Each tribe was divided into smaller bands.

Buffalo hunts often were very dangerous to the warriors and their horses.

The buffalo were central to the Lakota and Nakota way of life. Buffalo provided food, shelter, and clothing. The Lakota and Nakota followed buffalo herds across the plains. Each individual tribe had hunting grounds.

A Sioux warrior attempted to touch the enemy without hurting him. This accomplishment called "counting coup" was considered an act of great bravery.

Family Roles

Oceti Sakowin men and women were equals, but they each had very different roles. Lakota, Dakota, and Nakota men had two main roles as hunter and warrior. As hunters, men traveled in small groups to hunt buffalo or smaller game such as deer or elk. They used bows and arrows to kill the game.

Oceti Sakowin warriors traveled in war parties. A Lakota war party might fight a Crow war party for horses or hunting grounds. These battles often were called raids, because the warriors were raiding another tribe to steal their horses. A warrior sometimes used his bow, spear, or hand simply to touch the enemy. This attempt to show bravery was called counting coup. By counting coup, warriors won honors from their tribe rather than wounding or killing an enemy.

Lakota, Dakota, and Nakota women had a variety of roles. When a hunting party returned, women removed the hides and prepared the meat. They also made the hides into clothing and shelter. The women cut the meat into long, thin strips and hung it to dry in the sun. All foods not eaten immediately were dried for storage.

The women had other duties as well. They collected fruit and vegetables. They sewed their own designs on their clothing. When it was time to move, the women were in charge of packing. They took apart the tepee, which the Lakota spell "tipi." They folded all the tepee's furnishing together inside of it. All the household items belonged to the woman. At the new campsite, they set up the tepee again.

It was customary for an Oceti Sakowin man to have more than one wife. The main reason for this custom was because it was difficult for one woman to do all of the household chores alone. This custom also meant that the men needed to be great warriors and hunters to provide for more than one family. A man's second wife was often the first wife's sister. The first wife had to agree and approve of the second wife. Wives then shared duties, including raising the children.

At any time, men and women could divorce. A woman divorced her husband by setting his belongings outside the tepee or by leaving to live with her parents. A man could divorce his wife by beating a drum and announcing his decision to divorce her.

An entire village helped raise children. Storytelling was an important tool in teaching children about Oceti Sakowin history, customs, and values. Older people called elders told young children myths and legends that they had heard from their elders. Children learned how the Oceti Sakowin people came to be, about important battles, and about buffalo hunts.

A Oceti Sakowin woman is shown setting up a tepee at the Prairie Island Reservation in Minnesota. This picture was taken in 1903.

The stories taught children about bravery, courage, generosity, and wisdom.

Children did not go to school in a classroom. They learned by watching their parents and by playing games. Boys spent hours running races, practicing shooting with bows and arrows, and riding horses. Girls helped their mothers sew, cook, and clean. They played with toy dolls and sang familiar lullabies. These games and activities helped children train for the future.

Sun Dance

The wiwanyank waci, or Sun Dance, is one of the traditional spiritual ceremonies of the Oceti Sakowin. In historical times, it took place once each year, usually in the summer. In the ceremony, a band of Lakota, Dakota, or Nakota came together in one place to honor the creator, named Tunkasila, which means grandfather. Today, many Sun Dance ceremonies are held across the United States and Canada. Families prepare great feasts for the Sun Dance. People prepare to dance at the Sun Dance for different reasons. They might dance for the health of the people. They might dance for unity or in honor of someone.

During the Sun Dance, the person dances and prays without eating or drinking. In the past, some dancers made flesh offerings. Dancers could pierce the skin of their chest or back with two skewers made of buffalo bone. Each skewer was attached to a rope. The ropes were tied to a sacred pole, standing in the middle of the Sun Dance area.

The Sun Dance lasted four days. The dancers might not eat or sleep during this time. Dancers chose what they wanted to do. Dancers made a commitment on what they would sacrifice and took a year to prepare for the Sun Dance.

Warriors sometimes would endure great pain during the Sun Dance. The Sun Dance was a time for prayer.

The Sun Dance strengthened and united the tribe. The celebration honored bravery, generosity, and wisdom. The Oceti Sakowin treasured these values. By celebrating the Sun Dance, the Oceti Sakowin honored Tunkasila.

Quillwork

The Oceti Sakowin regarded quillwork as a special art. In quilling, a person sews porcupine quills on clothing to form designs. A young woman had to find an experienced elder to teach her the craft. To quill, women first held the quills in their mouths to wet and soften them. Women then used their teeth to flatten the quills before sewing them onto soft animal hide.

Quillers used natural and dyed quills. To dye porcupine quills, the quiller soaked bundles of quills in natural dyes, such as berry juice. After the bundle of quills dried, the quills had soaked up the color of the dye.

Quillwork was one of the many ways that Sioux women showed their creativity. They used natural dyes to dye porcupine quills used to decorate moccasins and other items.

Indian Fry Bread

White settlers introduced the Lakota to cooking ingredients such as baking powder and salt. Fry bread soon became a common food in the Lakota diet. This bread is good with honey or jam spread over it.

Ingredients:

3 cups (750 mL) flour
1 teaspoon (5 mL) baking powder
¼ teaspoon (1 mL) salt
1¼ cup (300 mL) water
¼ cup (50 mL) extra flour for kneading
¼ cup (50 mL) cooking oil
honey or jam for serving (if desired)

Equipment:

large mixing bowl
dry-ingredient measuring cups
measuring spoons
wooden mixing spoon
cutting board (or counter top)
large skillet
metal spatula

What you do:

1. In a large mixing bowl, combine flour, baking powder, and salt.
2. Use wooden mixing spoon to combine the ingredients and then push them to one side of the bowl.
3. Begin adding water while stirring ingredients.
4. Continue adding the water and stirring until the dough becomes stiff.
5. Sprinkle some of the extra flour on a cutting board or counter top.
6. With clean hands, remove the dough from the bowl and place it on the floured surface.
7. Knead the dough by pushing it with the heel of your hands, down and away from your body.
8. Rotate the dough one-quarter turn, fold the dough in half, and repeat.
9. Sprinkle additional extra flour if needed to keep the dough from sticking.
10. Continue to knead the dough until it is smooth and elastic.
11. Form flat, round bread patties. The patties should measure about 4 inches (10 centimeters) in diameter and be about ½ inch (1¼ centimeters) thick.
12. With adult supervision, heat cooking oil in skillet over medium heat.
13. Carefully place two or three of the bread patties into the hot oil.
14. Fry the bread about 2 minutes until the bottom side is brown.
15. Using a spatula, turn the bread and brown the other side.
16. Remove the cooked fry bread patties from pan with a spatula.
17. Continue steps 12 through 15 until all bread patties are cooked.
18. Serve with honey or jam.

Makes 8 to 10 bread patties.

The settlers brought supplies to distribute and trade to the Native Americans. Sioux Indians often traded furs and hides for supplies they needed.

Chapter Three

Who Are the Sioux?

Before 1841, the Oceti Sakowin spent little time with white people. The little contact they did have usually was friendly. The white people traded items such as knives, beads, and guns for animal furs and hides.

In 1841, the Oregon Trail opened. It was a route that led white settlers from Missouri to farmlands in present-day Oregon. Settlers began to cross through Dakota, Nakota, and Lakota lands on their way west. The U.S. government established a trading post called Fort Laramie along this route. Indian tribes from miles around rode to Fort Laramie to trade their buffalo hides for blankets, guns, needles, and other items they needed.

In 1848, white people discovered gold in California. Thousands of travelers crowded onto the Oregon Trail. The additional travelers scared away and killed the buffalo. They also brought new diseases such as smallpox, cholera, and

American Indians, traders, and soldiers visited Fort Laramie in Wyoming for supplies. Trading there became very popular when the Oregon Trail opened in 1841.

measles to the American Indians. Thousands of American Indians died from these diseases. Angry Indians started to raid the travelers, who grew frightened. White settlers asked the United States government to help them.

Fort Laramie Treaty of 1851

In 1851, the government organized the Fort Laramie Treaty Council. The purpose of this peace council was to get the Lakota to sign a treaty, or legal agreement. The government promised the Lakota plenty of gifts to convince them to attend. Around 10,000 Lakota people attended the meeting.

The treaty had several conditions. The Lakota would have to choose a single chief to speak for all Lakota tribes. They also had to live peaceably with whites and stop raiding white settlers. The United States would form territories for each of the tribes. Within that territory, the tribe could hunt freely. The United States would build roads and forts to help the settlers in their travels west.

If the Lakota agreed to sign the treaty, the United States promised to give them yearly gifts of food and supplies for a period of 50 years. Soldiers at the government forts would equally protect the rights of the American Indians and the white settlers.

The Lakota were not happy with the treaty conditions. They also had lived without defined territories for years. It was impossible to pick one leader for all of their people. Each individual band within a tribe had its own leader.

When the Lakota could not choose a single leader, the whites chose one for them. The whites chose Conquering Bear, a Brulé trade chief. Conquering Bear and a few other chiefs signed the treaty, but most did not think it would be possible to live by the treaty's terms.

Dakota Conflict of 1862

By 1860, the Dakota living in Minnesota were living on reservations. The U.S. government agreed through the Fort Laramie Treaty to supply them with food and supplies. Sometimes, supplies came months later than promised. Food often was rotten when it arrived. Government officials sometimes cheated the Dakota by not giving them as much food as promised.

In 1862, the Dakota fought back. First, a group of Dakota warriors broke into an agency store to take the supplies that were theirs according to the treaty. Thirteen days later, a Dakota warrior killed a white woman. In the weeks that followed, Dakota warriors killed more than 700 whites.

White settlers grew angry and demanded that the U.S. government punish the Dakota. The government sent most of the Dakota to reservations in Nebraska, North Dakota, and South Dakota. On December 26, 1862, authorities hanged 38 Dakota warriors in Mankato, Minnesota. It was the largest mass execution in U.S. history.

Dakota Indians attacked the town of New Ulm, Minnesota, during the Dakota conflict of 1862. The Dakota were fighting for supplies that the U.S. government had promised them.

Relations between the Lakota and the whites became more tense. Violence from both sides was becoming more frequent. White soldiers made surprise attacks on Indian tribes, including tribes that were known to be friendly.

General William Sherman and Commissioners had a meeting with Indian chiefs at Fort Laramie in Wyoming in 1868.

Fort Laramie Treaty of 1868

In 1866, the United States opened the Bozeman Trail from Wyoming to Montana, where gold had been discovered. This trail crossed directly through Lakota land. Lakota raided some settlers who tried to travel on the trail.

In 1868, government officials brought a treaty to Fort Laramie. The Fort Laramie Treaty of 1868 agreed that all of present-day South Dakota west of the Missouri River would become the Great Sioux Reservation. The Lakota would own this land forever. The treaty promised that government agencies on the reservation would supply the Lakota with food and clothing. The government also would teach the American Indians to farm and build them schools.

The land near the Powder River and the land west of the reservation would still be the Lakota's to hunt buffalo. No whites would be allowed to enter this region. Any chief who signed this treaty was promised gifts of food, clothing, tools, and money.

A few Red Cloud Lakota leaders agreed to sign this treaty with the U.S. government. Some waited until the Bozeman Trail was closed before signing to see if the government stood by its promises.

Battle of the Little Bighorn

In 1874, General George Armstrong Custer came to South Dakota. He and about 1,000 men were exploring the Black Hills. The United States had broken the Treaty of 1868. Many of the men who accompanied Custer hoped to strike it rich mining gold. Mining camps began to appear on Indian land. News of Custer's travels crossed the country. White settlers began to travel to the Black Hills in search of gold.

The U.S. government wanted to buy the Black Hills. Over the next year, the U.S. government tried to convince the Lakota to sell. Finally, the United States offered the Lakota $6 million for the land. The Lakota refused. The United States then ordered all Lakota chiefs, including those living in Powder River country, to reservations. Most chiefs and their tribes moved to reservations because they were tired of the fighting. Others did not move.

The government ordered soldiers to attack any American Indians who remained in the Black Hills. Lakota leaders, Crazy Horse and Sitting Bull, sent word to other Plains Indians to join them in defending the Black Hills. Thousands came to help. At the Battle of the Little Bighorn in 1876, Sitting Bull and Crazy Horse led a victory against Custer and the Seventh Cavalry. About 200 soldiers were killed.

The Plains Indians' victory over Custer greatly upset the government. More soldiers came into Lakota lands. They had orders to find any remaining Indians and forcibly take them to reservations. After years of running from soldiers, Sitting Bull and Crazy Horse finally surrendered and went to a reservation.

General George Armstrong Custer and the soldiers of the Seventh Cavalry fought with the Lakota and Cheyenne at the Battle of the Little Bighorn in Montana.

Crazy Horse

Crazy Horse was a Lakota warrior and leader. He was a quiet and modest warrior. He did not brag about his bravery and skill. He did not wear fancy headdresses, as many other warriors did. He often spent long hours alone.

In 1876, Crazy Horse helped lead his people to a victory in the Battle of the Little Bighorn. Crazy Horse continued to fight for his land until he finally surrendered to a reservation in 1877. On September 6, 1877, he was killed.

Ghost Dance and Wounded Knee

In the late 1880s, a new religion appeared among the Lakota and other Plains Indians. It was called the Ghost Dance religion. It encouraged American Indians to live peacefully and perform a ceremonial dance. In doing so, the American Indians would see the return of the buffalo and the disappearance of the white people.

White people were afraid of the Ghost Dance religion. They banned the practice of the religion. Chief Big Foot sought refuge at the Red Cloud Agency in South Dakota. He took along Lakota people. White settlers were stopped at Wounded Knee in present-day South Dakota and killed.

The U.S. government ordered the arrest of Chief Sitting Bull at the Standing Rock Reservation. Sitting Bull was killed during the arrest on December 15, 1890. Big Foot, another Lakota leader, fled after hearing of Sitting Bull's death.

On December 29, 1890, the U.S. Seventh Cavalry came to Wounded Knee to collect all the Lakota's weapons and to arrest Big Foot. It is not known who fired the first shot or even why it was fired. Some people believe it was an accident. Once the first shot rang out, soldiers opened fire on the Lakota. More than 300 Lakota died. This event became known as the Wounded Knee Massacre.

The Oceti Sakowin celebrated the Ghost Dance to bring peace, the return of the buffalo, and the disappearance of the white people.

Sioux children often attend events to learn about their heritage. This group of girls attended an event to celebrate their culture.

Chapter Four

Life in a Modern World

Dakota, Lakota, and Nakota people can be found across the United States and Canada. But most live in North and South Dakota, Minnesota, Montana, and Nebraska. Some live in the Canadian provinces of Manitoba and Saskatchewan. About half of the Lakota, Dakota, and Nakota people live off reservations in cities and towns.

On or off the reservation, Lakota children are similar to other American children. They wear T-shirts and blue jeans, watch TV, play video and computer games, go shopping, and spend time with their friends.

Education

From the 1880s to the 1970s, the U.S. government forced American Indian children to attend boarding schools. At these schools, Indians could not speak their native language. Teachers assigned them less "Indian-sounding" names. The children could not visit their families. They were forced to live at the boarding schools.

Since the 1970s, the government passed laws to protect American Indian children. They no longer go to boarding schools. Many Sioux Nation reservations now have tribal schools and colleges. Children learn about their history, culture, and language through native teachers. They also learn about the United States and world history, arts, sciences, and computers.

Economics

Many houses on Sioux reservations are run down and in need of repairs. Some do not have running water or electricity. They are located far from stores, banks, and schools. For these reasons, many Sioux choose to leave the reservation for big cities where they hope to find a better standard of living.

Some reservation housing is modern and similar to suburban cities. Tribal leaders are spending money to improve communities with new schools and hospitals. Some reservations have gambling casinos. The money that is made from the casinos pays for elder programs and education. The Sioux encourage new businesses in hopes of making communities bigger and more appealing.

In 1892, the student body assembled on the Carlisle Indian School Grounds in Carlisle, Pennsylvania. The Sioux often were forced to attend boarding schools.

Virginia Driving Hawk Sneve

In 1933, Virginia Driving Hawk Sneve was born on the Rosebud Reservation in South Dakota. She spent her childhood and teenage years there. She was the daughter of an Episcopal priest and a Lakota Sioux mother. After teaching English, Virginia began to write children's books. She has written more than 20 books, including fiction and nonfiction books. Sixteen of her books are about American Indians, based on her own background.

In 1992, Virginia Driving Hawk Sneve won the National Indian Prose Award. In 2000, she won the National Humanities Medal. This honor is given to people whose work has helped people to better understand the arts.

Health and Community Programs

Health conditions on reservations remain worse than in the rest of the United States. Diseases such as diabetes and alcoholism are common. Tribal leaders are working to improve these conditions. With improved education and better health care facilities, tribal leaders hope that the health of the Oceti Sakowin people will improve.

Many cities with large populations of Lakota, Dakota, or Nakota people have areas in which they gather. American Indian cultural centers are present in almost every large city. At the cultural centers, young people can learn about a particular tribe's history and culture. Native authors and artists sell books and artwork in the center's store. Elders come to the center to teach classes about crafts or language. Young and old people gather together to share their stories and experiences.

Tribal Government

The Lakota, Dakota, and Nakota nations follow the rules of each of their reservation's tribal governments. The laws set by these tribal governments are very similar to state or U.S. laws.

The people of each reservation elect a council and a tribal chairman. These people make the laws by which the people live. Each reservation has a tribal police department that enforces the laws.

A Lakota father often teaches his children about traditional customs and beliefs. He shares stories and takes his children to cultural events such as wacipis or powwows.

Chapter Five

Sharing the Old Ways

With the development of tribal schools on reservations, young children can learn about their culture and history. Children who live off the reservations often return with their families during the summer. They come to visit family and friends and attend social gatherings. During this time, children learn about traditional customs and beliefs.

Elders

Elders are one of the most important ways of passing on the Oceti Sakowin culture. Any person who has learned about traditional ways through experience or storytelling can pass that knowledge to the younger generation. Children gather information and learn to respect and value their elders.

Some American Indians and elders are sharing their knowledge through books and in schools. Children can learn

An old man demonstrates tribal traditions to the younger generation in this painting called *Dakota Teaching*.

about their culture and traditions through native writers. They also learn about Oceti Sakowin legends through books.

Wacipis

Oceti Sakowin people preserve their culture through wacipis. These gatherings, or powwows, feature a variety of events. Dancing has been a part of Oceti Sakowin culture for thousands of years. Long ago, dancers might have made a costume from the hide of a deer. The dancer would then dance using movements that looked like a deer. Today, this type of dancing is called traditional dancing.

Other kinds of dances are performed at powwows as well. Fancy-shawl dancing, gourd dancing, and jingle-dress dancing are some of the dances celebrated at wacipis.

Beadwork

White traders first introduced glass beads to American Indians, although the Indians used other beads before. Beading has become an important art form in many American Indian tribes. For more than 200 years, the Oceti Sakowin people have used beads to decorate clothing and other items used in ceremonies.

Today, some Oceti Sakowin people sell beaded items for income. Tourists can buy beadwork on jewelry, moccasins, and hats. Artists display and sell these works at local stores and craft fairs.

Sioux Timeline

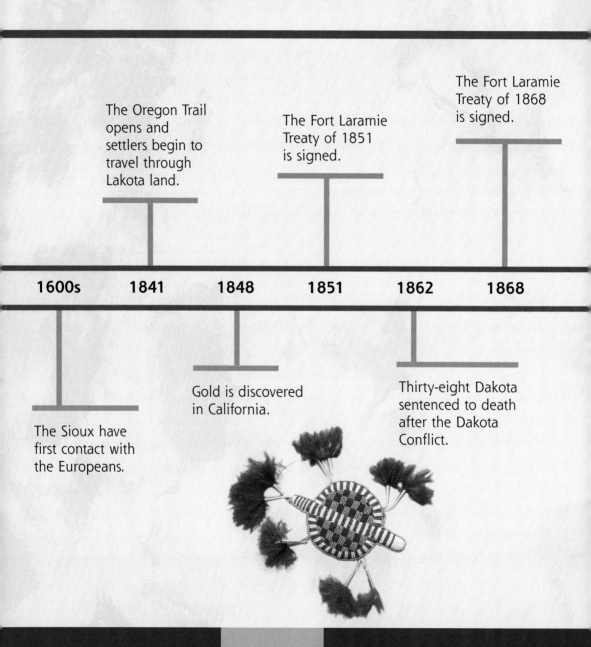

The Oregon Trail opens and settlers begin to travel through Lakota land.

The Fort Laramie Treaty of 1851 is signed.

The Fort Laramie Treaty of 1868 is signed.

1600s   1841   1848   1851   1862   1868

The Sioux have first contact with the Europeans.

Gold is discovered in California.

Thirty-eight Dakota sentenced to death after the Dakota Conflict.

The Battle
of the Little
Bighorn
is fought.

The Wounded Knee
Massacre takes place.

1874   **1876**   **1880s**   **1890**   **1970s**

General Custer
explores the
Lakota
homelands
located in the
Black Hills.

- The Ghost Dance
  Religion first starts.
- Lakota children are
  forced into
  boarding schools.

The Indian
boarding
schools close
down. New
tribal schools
open on
reservations.

Glossary

band (BAND)—a group of people, smaller than a tribe

cholera (KOL-ur-uh)—a disease that causes sickness and diarrhea

measles (MEE-zuhlz)—an easy-to-catch disease that causes fever, rash, and death

sacred (SAY-kred)—highly valued and important

smallpox (SMAWL-poks)—a very easy-to-catch disease that causes chills and high fevers and can leave scars

treaty (TREE-tee)—a legal agreement between nations

wacipi (wah-CHEE-pee)—a powwow

For Further Reading

Bial, Raymond. *The Sioux*. Lifeways. New York: Benchmark Books, 1999.

Press, Petra. *The Sioux*. First Reports Series. Minneapolis: Compass Point Books, 2001.

Rose, LaVera. *Grandchildren of the Lakota*. The World's Children. Minneapolis: Carolrhoda Books, 1999.

Santella, Andrew. *The Lakota Sioux*. A True Book. New York: Children's Press, 2001.

Places to Write and Visit

The Heritage Center
100 Mission Drive
Pine Ridge, SD 57770

Lower Sioux Agency Historic Site
32469 Redwood County Highway 2
Morton, MN 56270

South Dakota State Historical Society
900 Governors Drive
Pierre, SD 57501-2217

Internet Sites

A Guide to the Great Sioux Nation
http://www.travelsd.com/history/sioux/sioux.htm

The Lakota of the Plains
*http://www.carnegiemuseums.org/cmnh/exhibits/north-south-east
-west/lakota*

Native Peoples of Minnesota
http://emuseum.mnsu.edu/history/mncultures/nakota.html

Index